UNSOLVED

CAPTAIN KIDD'S TREASURE

DINAH WILLIAMS

Children's Press®

An imprint of Scholastic Inc.

Special thanks to our fact-checker M. L. Liu

Library of Congress Cataloging-in-Publication Data available

ISBN 978-1-5461-4160-0 (library binding) | ISBN 978-1-5461-4161-7 (paperback)

10 9 8 7 6 5 4 3 2 26 27 28 29

Printed in U.S.A. 150

First edition, 2025

Book design by Kay Petronio

Photos ©: back cover background: Granger Historical Picture Archive/Shutterstock; 2–3: Granger Historical Picture Archive/Shutterstock; 4: Look and Learn/Bridgeman Images; 5: Historia/Shutterstock; 6 inset: Doc Searls/Flickr; 8: Derek Bayes. All rights reserved 2024/Bridgeman Images; 10: Sunny Celeste/imageBROKER/Shutterstock; 11: Pobytov/Getty Images; 12: Reading Room 2020/Alamy Images; 14–15: Captain Kidd's Ship Adventure Galley; 16–17: Look and Learn/Bridgeman Images; 19: Look and Learn/Bridgeman Images; 20: William Gilkerson; 24: Historia/Shutterstock; 25, 27: North Wind Picture Archives/Alamy Images; 28–29: Look and Learn/Bridgeman Images; 30: Philip Game/Alamy Images; 31 foreground: Museum of the City of New York/Bridgeman Images; 32: Campwillowlake/Getty Images; 34: Jeremy Graham/Alamy Images; 35: Eileen Tweedy/Shutterstock; 37: Look and Learn/Bridgeman Images; 39: GL Archive/Alamy Images; 40: Margot Nicol-Hathaway/AP Images; 41: Martin Vogl-File/AP Images; 43: Giancarlo Costa/Bridgeman Images; 44 top left, 44 bottom: Look and Learn/Bridgeman Images; 44 top right: Geoff Lambertsen; 44 bottom left background: Hulton Archive/Getty Images; 45 top: Margot Nicol-Hathaway/AP Images; 45 top right background: IanDagnall Computing/Alamy Images; 45 bottom left: Philip Game/Alamy Images; 45 bottom right: Manjakahery Tsiresena/AFP/Getty Images; 46 top: Wikimedia; 46 center: Dorling Kindersley/Getty Images; 46 bottom: RobertKacpura/Getty Images.

All other photos © Shutterstock.

CONTENTS

INTRODUCTION: The Lost Treasure 4

CHAPTER 1: Kidd Sets Sail 8

CHAPTER 2: Hunted Pirate 20

CHAPTER 3: Hidden Treasure 32

CHAPTER 4: What to Believe? 42

Timeline: Then and Now 44

More Pirate Treasure Hunts 46

Glossary 47

Index 48

About the Author 48

THE LOST TREASURE

Pirates are criminals of the seas. They attack ships carrying **goods**. They steal the ships and sometimes kill the crew. There were many pirates about three hundred years ago. Sailors had to keep constant watch over their ships.

There are no photographs of Captain Kidd. This is probably what he looked like.

Captain Kidd was one of the most famous pirates. He was a pirate hunter turned pirate. He captured many ships filled with **loot**. Kidd eventually became wanted by the law. He had to bury his treasure to keep it safe. But where did he hide it?

A drawing of Captain Kidd's treasure. The chest has the initials "W. K." for William Kidd.

Gardiner's Island is a small island in New York State. It sits at the east end of Long Island.

We know some of Captain Kidd's treasure was buried at Gardiner's Island. A chest of gold, silver, and jewels was later recovered. But what happened to the rest of his riches?

Legend says Kidd had more loot that was never found. Where was it buried? Treasure hunters are still searching for it today! Let's explore what we know about this mystery.

CHAPTER 1

KIDD SETS SAIL

This is a painting of Kidd as a young man.

William Kidd was born in Scotland around 1645. He worked on ships like his father did. There is not much known about his early life.

We do know that Kidd sailed to the **Caribbean** in 1689. He and the rest of the crew staged a **mutiny** during the trip. This meant they stole the ship from the captain. They named the ship *Blessed William* after the English king. The crew made Kidd the new captain.

KIDD'S EARLY YEARS

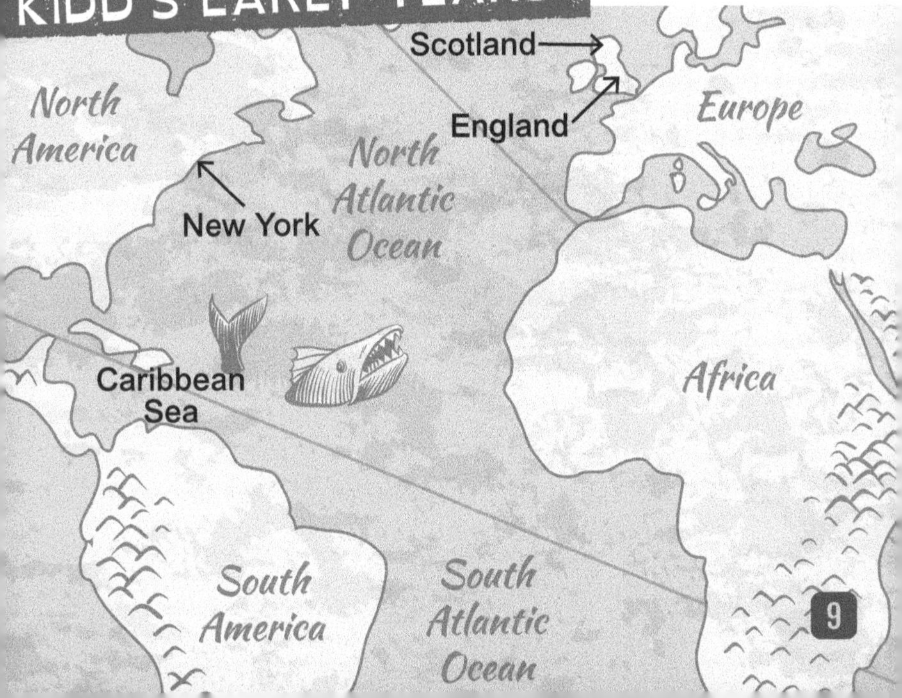

This painting shows Captain Kidd holding hands with a woman. Some people think it is his wife, Sarah.

Kidd and the *Blessed William* joined the British Navy. They helped the British fight the French in the Caribbean. But they were not paid for fighting. The British said they could steal from the French to earn money. So Kidd attacked a French town. They stole all of the loot they could carry.

The British gave Kidd a reward. He settled in New York City. In 1691, he married one of the richest women in the city. Her name was Sarah Oort. They had two daughters.

ROBERT CULLIFORD

About a year later, a pirate stole the *Blessed William* from Kidd. His name was Robert Culliford. Kidd and Culliford would cross paths again.

The *Blessed William* looked similar to the pirate ship shown here.

This is the Earl of Bellomont. His actual name was Richard Coote.

British ships were being harassed by pirates. The British were still at war with France. In 1695, Kidd joined forces with the Earl of Bellomont. Kidd agreed to hunt pirates and attack French ships.

Bellomont would later become the governor of New York. He reported to the king of England. He was part of a powerful group of British men. They would help pay for a new ship for Kidd. Kidd thought he could make a lot of money.

HAUNTED GRAVEYARD

After Kidd was married, he helped with the construction of Trinity Church. The church is located in New York City. Kidd planned to be buried there. Some say Kidd's ghost haunts the church's graveyard.

This is the graveyard at Trinity Church.

Kidd's new ship, *Adventure Galley*, was built to catch pirates. It cost a lot of money to construct. It had thirty-four cannons and was big enough for 150 men. What made it special was its oars. They could move the ship when there was no wind for the sails. But Kidd needed to find a crew.

Kidd didn't have enough money to pay sailors. So, he hired them with a promise of payment instead. They would get a piece of any loot captured. Kidd also had to pay back the British for the boat. He needed to find pirates to make any money.

The *Adventure Galley* cost about one million US dollars in today's money to build.

A skull and crossbones on a black flag signaled an attack. Kidd kept watch for pirate flags like this one.

The *Adventure Galley* set sail in 1696. Kidd quickly captured a French ship. He was off to a good start. He headed toward the Indian Ocean. He was ready to begin pirate hunting. But that is where Kidd's luck ran out.

He sailed for a year without capturing any pirate ships. The *Adventure Galley* was leaking. It needed new sails. A number of the crew died from disease. Food was running out. The crew was whispering about a mutiny.

One of Kidd's crew, William Moore, spotted a **Dutch** ship. He and the crew wanted to attack it. But it was not French nor a pirate ship. So, Kidd refused.

Moore was angry. Kidd called him a lousy dog. Moore said, "If I am a lousy dog, you have made me so. You have brought me to ruin." Kidd was furious! He threw a bucket at Moore's head. The blow killed Moore. Kidd was now a criminal!

Captain Kidd about to strike William Moore with a bucket.

CHAPTER 2

HUNTED PIRATE

The hideout Kidd stopped at in Madagascar was a headquarters for pirates.

The ship sailed on. Kidd's luck finally changed in 1698. He captured two more ships. They appeared to be French. They were packed with riches. He named one *November* and the other *Adventure Prize*. Kidd took the ships to a pirate hideout in Madagascar.

There, about half of Kidd's crew left. They wanted to make more money. They joined Robert Culliford. He was the pirate who had stolen from Kidd before. The crew took the *November* to Culliford. Kidd didn't have many sailors left.

MADAGASCAR

Madagascar is an island country off the coast of Africa.

The *Adventure Galley* was too leaky to sail. Kidd emptied it and set it on fire. He and his small crew watched it sink. He set off on the *Adventure Prize*. Kidd didn't know what trouble awaited him.

The original name of *Adventure Prize* was *Quedagh Merchant*.

The captain of one of the French ships he stole was English. Most of the cargo was owned by the English East India Company. News of the ship's capture had reached England. Kidd was now wanted as a pirate!

Kidd learned that the British Navy wanted to arrest him. They were looking for the *Adventure Prize*. Kidd hid the ship in the Caribbean Sea. He sold off some of the goods he had stolen. He kept chests of gold, silver, and jewels. He sailed on another ship back to New York in 1699.

He stopped at Gardiner's Island. He paid a family to bury some of his treasure on their land. The spot was marked on a map. He hoped the hidden treasure would convince Bellomont to help him.

Kidd landing on Gardiner's Island with his riches.

BURIED TREASURE?

In movies, pirates are often shown burying their treasure. But that didn't happen often in real life. Captain Kidd was one of the few who did this.

Kidd ordering his men to bury treasure under the moonlight.

Kidd made his way to New York City. He didn't know Bellomont was in Boston. Kidd spent some time with his wife and daughters. He then set sail for Boston. Bellomont promised he would not arrest Kidd. But he lied. Kidd was arrested as soon as he arrived.

Kidd told Bellomont that the ships he captured were French. He had papers to prove it. He also told him about the treasure on Gardiner's Island. It didn't help. Kidd was sent to England to stand trial.

DIGGING UP TREASURE

Bellomont ordered Kidd's treasure to be dug up on Gardiner's Island. There were bags filled with gold, silver, and jewels. But it was not everything that had been on Kidd's ship.

Men digging for Kidd's pirate treasure.

Pirates had become a huge problem for the British. The government decided to make an example of Kidd. He was held in prison for almost two years. Kidd didn't meet his lawyers until the day of his trial.

Before his trial, Kidd said he would hand over his hidden treasure. In exchange, he would be released. Was he telling the truth about his riches? Or was Kidd just trying to save himself?

He learned his papers proving he had captured French ships were gone. He also learned he was being charged with killing William Moore. Kidd was quickly found guilty of **piracy** and murder. He was sentenced to death.

Kidd was hanged on May 23, 1701. The rope broke on the first try. The crowd yelled that it was a sign. Kidd must be innocent! But he was hanged again and died.

Kidd's body was placed in an iron cage. It was hung over the Thames River in London, England. His body was left there for three years as a warning to other pirates.

These are stairs leading to the Thames River. Kidd's body was left near this spot.

GHOST STORY

Over a hundred years after Kidd died, a legend began. It was about two US soldiers who were assigned to Bedloe's Island. Kidd had lived near there while in New York. Maybe his treasure was buried on the island? The soldiers started searching. One night, they dug up a heavy metal box. Kidd's angry spirit shot out. It threw one of the soldiers into the box. The other soldier ran away. The treasure was never found.

Bedloe's Island later became Liberty Island. It is now home to the Statue of Liberty.

CHAPTER 3

HIDDEN TREASURE

Kidd thanking Mercy Raymond with some of his riches.

Mercy Raymond lived on Block Island. It is located off the coast of Rhode Island. She told a story that convinced people there was more treasure. Kidd and his wife had visited her in the 1690s. He asked if his wife could stay with Mercy's family. Mercy said yes.

Kidd left and picked up his wife weeks later. He told Mercy to hold out her apron. He filled it with handfuls of gold and jewels. The Raymond family later bought hundreds of acres of land in Connecticut.

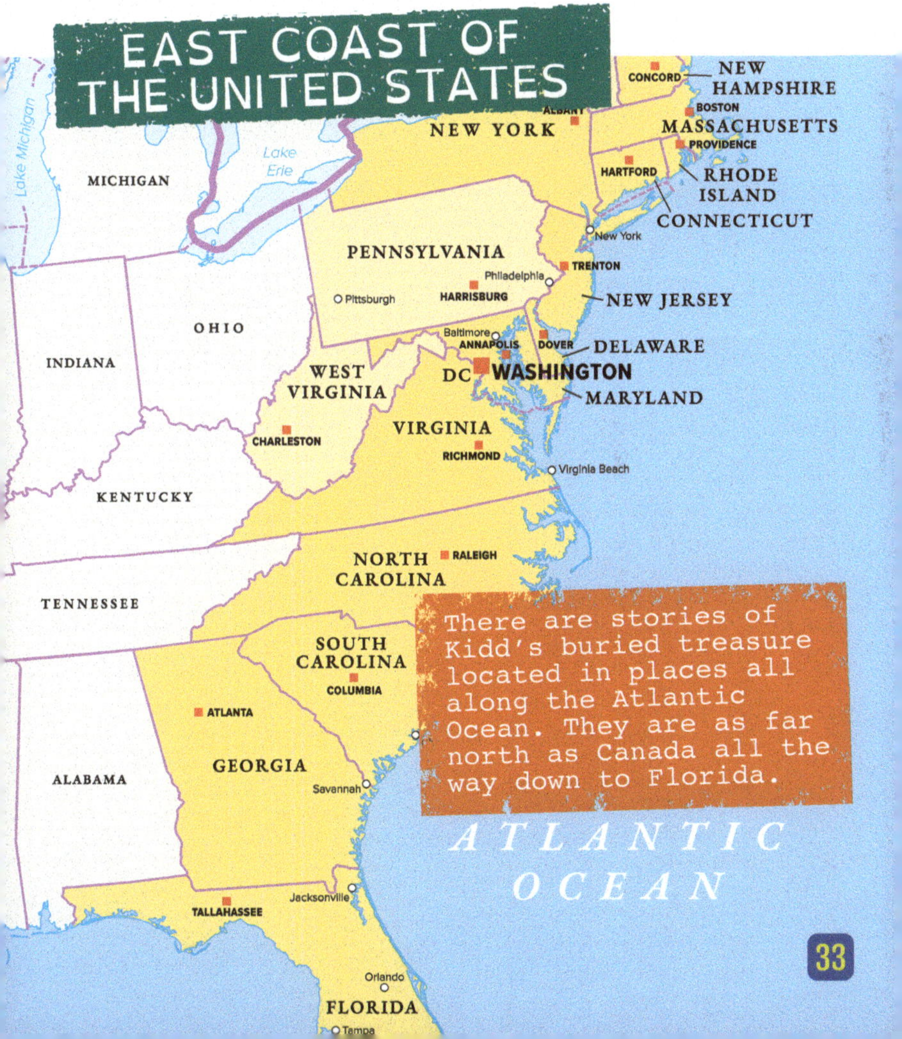

There are stories of Kidd's buried treasure located in places all along the Atlantic Ocean. They are as far north as Canada all the way down to Florida.

But where is the rest of Kidd's treasure? Kidd was also said to have stopped in the Thimble Islands. These are a large group of islands off the coast of Connecticut.

One of these islands has a cave. Some people think Kidd hid some of his treasure there. But it has never been found.

Thimble Islands

Kidd sailed the *Saint Antonia* into Delaware Bay in 1699.

Kidd also stopped in Delaware Bay for ten days in 1699. He sent his men to the nearby town of Lewes to get supplies. Kidd invited the local people onto his ship. They reported seeing the treasures he had brought back.

Some believe Kidd buried gold coins at Delaware Bay beach. A giant stone was found there in 1890 with a *K* carved in it. But Kidd's treasure was never recovered.

Piracy was common in Delaware Bay in the late 1600s.

The Hudson River runs through New York State. It's possible Kidd buried some of his treasure along it.

Kidd was said to have made other stops on his way to New York. He was worried Bellomont would have him arrested. Some say he buried treasure along the coast. He didn't want the law to take his money.

Some think he stopped somewhere in North Carolina. He buried loot on a small island there. He paid one of his crew to watch over his fortune. The man dug up what he could find after Kidd died. He then moved to Charleston a rich man. Gold coins were later found on the island.

The place Kidd buried his loot is called Money Island. This replica of a pirate ship is sailing near there.

TREASURE ISLAND

Robert Louis Stevenson's *Treasure Island* is a famous book. It was based in part on Captain Kidd and his buried treasure.

The shipwreck of the *Adventure Galley* was claimed to be found in 2000. A team of divers discovered it off the coast of Madagascar. They dove to the wreck several times. They found pottery and old bottles of **rum**.

Barry Clifford is an American explorer. He led both teams of divers in 2000 and 2015.

Clifford holding what was thought to be a bar of silver.

Fifteen years later, divers searched the wreck again. They found a 110-pound bar of silver. Treasure at last! But the bar was later tested. It was lead, not silver. It was probably used to weigh down the ship as it sailed.

CHAPTER 4

WHAT TO BELIEVE?

Captain Kidd was once a wealthy man. He was also a successful pirate hunter. He buried one treasure that was discovered. But where did he hide the rest of his riches? Treasure hunters are still trying to solve the mystery.

Without enough evidence, the mystery may remain unsolved. What do you believe? Maybe you're not sure. Maybe Captain Kidd's lost treasure will never be found!

Would you ever look for buried treasure?

TIMELINE: Then and Now

Kidd sets sail on the *Adventure Galley* to hunt pirates.

Kidd captures a ship he believes is French.

1696 1697 1698

Kidd kills William Moore.

The wreck of the *Adventure Galley* is found.

1701	2000	2015

Kidd is hanged for murder and piracy in England.

A huge lead bar is found at the wreck.

MORE PIRATE TREASURE HUNTS

Captain Kidd isn't the only pirate whose treasure has never been found. Here are a few more!

Amaro Pargo was a successful Spanish pirate. He died in 1747. He wrote in his will about a wooden chest. It was filled with jewels and gold. But no one has ever been able to find it.

English pirate Edward Teach was also known as Blackbeard. Before he died in 1718, he said his real treasure was hidden. Blackbeard said "no Body but himself and the Devil knew where it was." People have been looking for it ever since.

Twelve chests of treasure were stolen by pirates in Lima, Peru, in 1820. The captain was caught but escaped before he revealed the location. The treasure has never been found.

GLOSSARY

Caribbean (kuh-RIB-ee-uhn) or (kar-uh-BEE-uhn) the sea near the Atlantic Ocean, between North and South America. The Caribbean contains many small islands

Dutch of or relating to the Netherlands or its people

goods (gudz) things that are sold or things that someone owns

loot items that have been stolen or taken by force

mutiny (MYOO-tuh-nee) a revolt against or refusal to obey authority, especially in the military

piracy (PYE-ruh-see) the crime of attacking and robbing ships at sea

rum (ruhm) an alcoholic drink made from sugarcane

INDEX

A
Adventure Galley, 14–20, 22, 40–41, 44–45
Adventure Prize, 20, 22–24
B
Bedloe's Island, 31
Bellomont, Earl of, 12, 24, 26–27, 37
Blackbeard, 46
Blessed William, 9–11
Block Island, 32
British Navy, 10, 12, 24
C
Caribbean, 9–10, 24
Clifford, Barry, 40, 41
Culliford, Robert, 11, 21
D
Delaware Bay, 35–36
Dutch ships, 18
F
flags, 17
French ships, 12, 16, 23, 26, 29, 44
G
Gardiner's Island, 6, 24, 26–27
ghosts, 13, 31
goods, 4, 24
J
Jolly Roger, 17
K
Kidd, Captain William
  early life of, 8–9
  family of, 10, 26, 32–33
  as pirate hunter, 12, 14–16, 20, 44
  ships captured by, 12, 16, 20, 23, 26, 29, 44
  trial and hanging of, 26, 28–30, 45
Kidd's treasure
  burying of, 5, 24–25
  discovery of, 6, 27, 42
  locations of, 5–7, 24, 31–38
  searches for, 7, 31, 40–41, 45
L
loot, 5, 7, 10, 15, 38
M
Madagascar, 20–21, 40
Money Island, 38
Moore, William, 18–19, 29, 44
mutiny, 9, 17
N
November, 20, 21
O
Oort, Sarah, 10, 26, 32–33
P
Pargo, Amaro, 46
piracy charges, 29, 4
pirates, defined, 4
R
Raymond, Mercy, 32–33
rum, 40
S
Stevenson, Robert Louis, 39
T
Teach, Edward, 46
Thimble Islands, 34

ABOUT THE AUTHOR

Dinah Williams, who loves all things spooky and mysterious, has written more than a dozen books for kids, including *Amazing Immortals*; *Terrible But True: Awful Events in American History*; *True Hauntings: Deadly Disasters*; and *Spooky Cemeteries*, which wor a 2009 Children's Choice Book of the Year Award.